IMPASSIONED INTENTIONS

SHANICEXLOLA

INTRODUCTION

Impassioned Intentions is a steamy, emotional novel-ette with a beginning, middle and end. If longer books are your preference, please indulge in another ShanicexLola read.

*Please note, the poem performed in this book, *When I Look at You*, was written by K. Giles. It is from her collection of poetry entitled, *Love to Me is*.

DISCLOSURE

Before you proceed, please note that some parts of this novelette are arousing, adventurous, and down-right raunchy. I encourage you to read with an open mind to thoroughly enjoy the passion within.

xoxo, ShanicexLola

SYNOPSIS

He couldn't complete me. In fact, he refused to.

He struggled to figure me out, and I didn't know how to help him put the pieces of my complex puzzle together.

I couldn't bring him down with me. In fact, I refused to.

I struggled to let him love me, and he didn't know how to stop proving he did.

Love. We hit it hard.

I will be my own fucking hero.

PROLOGUE

So, this is how it happened.

Whipping into the parking lot of my bullshit ass job, I considered quitting as I searched for an available space. Every time I thought I found one, a motorcycle proved me wrong. In my opinion, all of the bikers in the building needed to park together, only taking up a few spaces instead of several spaces throughout the lot.

What was the point of a suggestion box or the surveys the company sent out if they weren't going to listen to their employees' opinions?

Like I said, my job was bullshit.

Gnawing on the side of my bottom lip, I punched the steering wheel, then sped into the first available parking space I came up on. From where I sat, the space looked over a couple thousand feet away from the entrance but screw it. Maybe the extra steps would help me burn off the calories from the four too many waffles I'd drowned in maple syrup this morning.

After snatching my purse from the backseat, I grabbed my Strawberry Cream Grande from my cup holder—the reason I was twenty minutes late in the first place. Thank God I'd stopped for it. I needed something cool to sip on until I got inside the building and escaped the beaming sun.

"It never fails," someone shouted out to me from the opposite end of the massive parking lot. I could've recognized that deep, raspy voice in any setting and at any time. "Yo thick ass is always late," my work husband, Dru, said. Him and his long legs reached me in no time at all.

Draping his heavy arm around my shoulder, Dru chuckled at my tardiness, showing off his beautiful, pearly whites in the process. Besides his deep pockets, his beautiful teeth that formed a perfect smile was the best thing he had going for himself. Then came the way he always smelled good and dressed to impressed. Being his work wife came with nice, exclusive benefits. Like free lunch, random gifts on my desk when I arrived at work, and around-the-clock snacks while I was clocked in.

"I wouldn't be surprised if they try to walk you out today," he said, using his badge to get us in the building. At the sight of his badge, I remembered that I'd forgotten mine on my kitchen counter.

"You gonna riot for me if they do, right?" I bat my long lashes and wrapped my slender arm around his tall, stocky body.

"Damn right, baby," he answered quickly. He always did. Dru wanted a deeper relationship with me. One that wasn't limited to work or deemed an ongoing joke between us.

"See you at lunch?" I asked, prepared to part ways.

Dru worked in a different department of the call-center than me. And thank God he did. Before he'd gotten promoted from taking calls to working on chats and emails, we were on the same team. Our cubicles were right next to each other and he took advantage of that every chance he got.

"See me wherever you want, girl." He winked, licked his ashy lips, then started in the opposite direction.

I rolled my eyes at how corny he could be sometimes. My amusement transformed into a frown because my brand-new flats were too tight around my toes. They needed to be broken into and today was the wrong day for that.

"You're late, Ms. Nicholson," my boss stood from the seat behind his desk, announcing my arrival.

"Can't get anything past you, Mr. Finch." His cubicle was at the end of his 12-member team. Standing, he hovered over our section, just like he hovered over the way we did our jobs.

I rolled my eyes at him as he scanned our area, double-checking that everyone was doing their part. His headset covered his elf ears and he was probably listening to someone's live call. I didn't put anything past his overbearing, micromanaging ass.

"Don't get comfortable," he said, stopping me before I plopped down onto my seat. "The calls are slow today. I'm putting you on the MTO list."

"I don't want to be MTO'd. I rather work."

"You've been late every day this week. Every team lead on this floor has to MTO three people from their team today because it's slow. Since you were late, it's only fair for you to go home."

"You can't be serious! If that's the case, you could've called and told me that before I got here."

Finch stared at me without blinking. His golden, beady eyes zoomed in on my light brown face, then bounced over it. I balled my fist, envisioning knocking him cross-eyed. No one irritated me more at work than Finch. Not even the bratty customers. His abrasive, cocky demeanor triggered my feminism. The way he walked around like him, his dick, and his balls owned the building made me want to start a riot around his cubicle with colorful signs that reminded him he wasn't shit—signs that reminded him he only made a few dollars more than the team members under him.

"Whatever." I straightened my posture and situated my purse over my arm. Storming away from him, I took a sip from my drink, trying to cool down the fire brewing inside of me.

Some of my coworkers grumbled and voiced their complaints about him sending me home. Diana, an older woman who'd deemed me her work daughter, offered to go home in my place. I dismissed everything everyone said by walking in the opposite direction. Hopefully they didn't take it personally. I needed to get away from Finch before I let loose on him.

I sensed someone trailing me out of the building, and I assumed we were exiting in pairs since team leads were sending agents home. That was the bullshit I didn't like about call centers. Well, my ongoing list was pretty long. However, the unknown of the incoming traffic was bothersome. It also depended on the season.

Working at Fandango's call center was nerve-wrecking. One day, calls would be through the roof and mandatory overtime was dispersed to all the agents. Other days, agents were being forced to go home and accept mandatory time off.

Who knew people were so damn hot and cold when it came down to seeing movies?

Good thing I had a side hustle, or I'd be living in my parent's basement. They'd turned my old room into a storage unit, so that wasn't an available option for me.

Yanked in the opposite direction, I was snatched into a pitch-black janitor's closet and locked inside. Feeling around for a light switch, my back was pressed against the wall before I discovered it.

"Quinton, I don't have time for this. You just sent me home and that's where I want to be right now."

"You know I had to."

"You didn't have to do sh—"

Rudely interrupted by a kiss, he embraced me tightly, holding my body close to his as he grumbled in my ear.

"Don't make this harder on me than it already is."

His large hands gripped my hips, then roamed down my back until he slapped and squeezed my ass cheeks.

"People are starting to get suspicious of us. I can't reward you for being late, no matter how good you look when you arrive." His full lips blessed my cheek, then he gently kissed the side of my lips.

I couldn't stand Mr. Finch when he was clocked into work, taking his position too seriously. But I was in love with Quinton Finch when we were wrapped up in each other. I was dangerously in love with him whenever he put me first. Right now, he was risking his job for me. My clit pulsated for him to have me. My body physically ached because it'd been over twelve hours since I felt him deeply inside of me.

"Screw those people," I murmured against his lips. "I'm tired of you putting them before me."

He pulled back from me. The closet was pitch black, and in this moment, I was grateful I couldn't witness his disappointed scowl. "Why do you say things like that to piss me off, J? You know damn well no one comes before you." Closing in on me again, he snarled in my ear, practically growling his disdain over my latest comment. "What do you want me to do?"

I wished I could see him tower over me. His full

beard rubbed lightly against my skin, making my body quiver. I reached up and caressed his smooth cheek. The darkness didn't stop me from visualizing his dark brown skin. His exclusive melanin was one of my favorite things about him.

"Nothing," I whispered, snatching my hand away. "You need to get back to work, and I don't want to be in this building any longer if I'm not getting paid for it."

I didn't know what I wanted.

"Figure it out," he said, pinning me against the wall again. He unbuttoned my slacks, and I let him. Despite how much I wanted to push him away and distance myself from the confusion of our situation-ship, I smashed my body into his. I let my pants fall to my ankles and panted as he tore the thin strap on my panties, ripping them off of me. He groped my breasts through my loose, pale-blue blouse.

"Quinton," I moaned, then gasped as he entered me. With my leg around his waist, he squeezed my hips, stroking deeply inside of me.

Quitting him was going to be harder than I thought.

BACK AT HOME, I paced around my house like it was the first night I'd moved in all over again. Back and forth down my long, narrow hallway, I counted backwards from ten, trying to settle down my anxiety.

"You can do this, Jana," I mumbled to myself.

The timer that had been counting down for twenty-four hours was running out. I only had a half an hour left before I was set to perform live in front of my YouTube subscribers—ten-thousand subscribers to be precise. They'd never seen my face, but they'd heard my voice and witnessed my fingers glide across my piano keys with ease. In a little under six months, an organic audience of ten-thousand people had flocked to my YouTube account after only three videos.

Whether they saw my face or not, performing in front of others didn't get easier. The number of uploads didn't matter. If it wasn't necessary, I wouldn't even do it. These days, it was the only thing that helped me feel better. Performing in front of strangers who resonated with the pain in my voice lessened the tension on my heart.

Flipping my shoulder-length, jet-black curls out of my face, I hummed the melody to the song I planned on singing. Brushing my fingers along the keyboard, I stared ahead at the countdown on my

MacBook desktop monitor, then closed my eyes and aired a deep breath.

Before I knew it, I only had five minutes left to freak out and then calm down my erratic breathing. It was time to express myself the best way I knew how. By covering songs that best described my feelings and thought process.

Bing!

The countdown was over, and a red light confirmed that I was officially live.

The camera was positioned on my hands and keyboard. Not only did I not want to risk my features being noticed by someone who would recognize me, I didn't want my raw emotions captured on screen. Only through my voice would I allow my pain to expose my true feelings.

"Hello, beautiful people. Thank you so much for joining my live stream. I truly appreciate all the support and love you all have shown me." I chuckled awkwardly while at a loss for words for a few seconds. Those few seconds felt like five long minutes. "I'll never be able to thank you enough for your kind comments, donations, subscriptions and likes. You guys really don't have to donate anything," I said, as a twenty-dollar donation alert popped up on my screen. "Just..." I sighed and played a simple tune on my keyboard to warm up. "Thank you for everything."

All of the, *you're welcome* and *you deserve it,* replies warmed my heart and made me comfortable enough to get started. After clearing my throat, I tilted my head to the right and channeled a load of boss bitch energy.

"*I tried to talk to my piano. I tried and tried and tried some more. Told secrets 'til my voice was sore. Tired of empty conversation, 'cause no one hears me anymore.*" I paused singing to gather my composure. My emotions were tumbling down quickly.

"*Anyone,*" I belted out. "*Please send me anyone. Lord is there anyone? I need someone.*" My throat vibrated as tears welled in my eyes. I stroked each appropriate key on the piano with power from my fingertips. If the keyboard was fragile, it would've snapped in half.

"*I used to crave the world's attention. I think I cried too many times. I just need some more affection. Anything to get me by.*" Tears cascaded down my high cheekbones, and I let them flow freely. I sniffled in the middle of a lyric, allowing my tears to fall onto the keyboard.

"*A hundred million stories and a hundred million songs, I feel stupid when I sing. Nobody's listening to* me. *Nobody's listening. I talk to shooting stars, but they always get it wrong. I feel stupid when I pray. Why the fuck am I praying anyway? If nobody's listening.*"

At the end of my performance, I opened my eyes to dozens of comments flowing on my screen. Some of my viewers told me they were crying with me, while others sent me hearts and sweet, encouraging sentiments. After thanking them, I ended the live and crawled onto one of the beanbag chairs in the corner of my office. The relief that overcame me was exhilarating. Despite how difficult it was to put myself out there like that, it felt damn good doing it.

Twenty minutes later, a knock at my front door, followed by my doorbell ringing, told me exactly who was visiting me. My older sister only used her spare key for emergencies, which was all the time. She must've been in a *patient* mood today—a trait she lacked, but a mood she displayed every other month.

"Girl, come on in and stop playing," I shouted from my office. It was the closest room to the front door and the window was partially open, so I knew she heard me.

A minute later, she was plopping down onto the beanbag chair next to me. Per usual, her thick, long hair was in a tight ponytail on top of her head. Like mine, her sandy brown skin, hazel eyes and deep dimples mirrored our father's features. Looking into her face always made me think of him.

"What are you doing here?" I smiled at her chinky eyes. I didn't understand her fascination with having her ponytail high and super tight at all times. Whenever I asked her about it, she reminded me that beauty was pain. She liked Ariana Grande a little too much.

"Dang. A girl just can't visit her little sister to see how she's doing?"

"The girl in front of me only does that when she thinks something is wrong."

Monae shrugged. "You haven't posted any baking tutorials on your Insta-story lately. Is something wrong?"

"There's some fresh white macadamia nut cookies in the kitchen, if that's what you're asking me. Made them when I got in from work."

"Hold that thought." She hopped up from the beanbag chair and dashed out of the doorway.

"Bring me a some too," I shouted behind her. "And a bottle of water!"

In less than five minutes, she returned with a small, plastic container of cookies and two bottles of water.

"Now back to you, Jana Monae," she said, plopping back down onto the beanbag chair.

I rolled my eyes and snickered. Our mother really thought she did the damn thing when she gave us each other's first name as our middle names.

"Monae Jana, I am fine, I assure you."

"Okay. Okay." She stuffed her mouth with a cookie, then lifted her hands to surrender. "But you know we're here for you, right?" she asked, side-eyeing me. She included our brother, Monty, in all of our serious conversations. Not only was he her twin, she took our family's closeness seriously.

"We know you've been going through a tough time trying to figure out your purpose and what direction you're—"

"Mo," I interrupted her while biting off a chunk from my cookie. "I love you both. I know I can get through anything with y'all by my side. I'll be okay."

"You'll be okay? Or, are you okay? Which one is it?" She swallowed hard, then set her cookies aside. "Look, Jana, you're twenty-nine and you're just getting started. You don't have to have it all figured out right now."

"Easy for you to say. You have the successful accounting career you've talked about having since we were teenagers. You're happily married with three beautiful triplets, who you need to stop coming over here without, by the way. I don't get to see my nieces enough." I pouted. "Your life is complete. You're fulfilled in all areas."

"Oh, sweetie, you can take your nieces off my hands whenever you want. All they do is ask about you anyway." She rolled her eyes, visibly hating on my tight bond with my nieces. They admired me just as much as I adored them. "I don't know what's going on with your new obsession with age, and getting older, but I wish you would cut it out. So what you said you would be married with kids and have it all figured out by the time you were thirty? I'm pushing thirty-five and don't have shit figured out just yet. That's life.

Terrance and I said we would own a huge home by now. We planned our lives together back when we were in high school and nothing happened the way we said it would. We had the girls unexpectedly. We still live in a two-bedroom apartment. We make good money, but our student loans are overwhelming us. The list goes on, girl. Don't be fooled by what you think is going on in people's lives. Everyone struggles in their own way, and everyone goes through this bullshit phase you're going through. Don't let your mind psych you out. Remind yourself that you got this, because you do."

"You done?" I quipped. Monty had given me a similar speech last week. I understood what they were trying to get through to me, but it was all easier said than done, of course.

"Girl." She balled her fist, shaking it in front of me. "You better listen to me. I know a little something."

"Thank you." I crawled over to her, wrapping my arms around her neck. "I do listen to you. I look up to you. I love you," I whispered, holding back tears that welled up in my eyes.

"I love you too, sis." She kissed my cheek. "You will find your way." She stated it like she wholeheartedly believed it. Little did she know, I didn't know which way to turn to find it. Shit, I hardly knew if I was headed in the right direction.

Just like her, I didn't know what was going on with my new obsession with age and getting older. All I knew was, something was missing in my life. I wanted more, I deserved more, and I didn't know where to start with going after it.

CHAPTER 1

QUINTON FINCH CORNERED me against the wall in my living room. The moment I opened the front door and invited him inside, he slammed the door behind him, locked it and then trapped me between his arms.

I loved me some him, and he had no idea. Or maybe he did. We'd worked at Fandango's call center for years, but we'd minded our business and kept our eyes on our own computer screens until we wound up in an unorganized meeting together. A meeting that could've been condensed to an email put us together. He'd sat down in an available seat next to me and looked over at me.

Once he did a double take, we locked eyes and his golden, beady eyes did a spell on me. After our meeting, he searched my name in the system and instant messaged me. I agreed to dinner after work and he was lying between my thighs for dessert. That was three months ago. I'd spent three months trying to hold back and talk myself out of falling in love with him.

Jokes on me.

Quinton Finch rocked my world.

As if things weren't already complex between us, him being promoted to a team lead position and becoming my boss took the cake.

After he inhaled me, he released a deep breath and slapped his hand on the wall. "I needed that," he mumbled in my ear. He always reminded me that I was his fix, and he was so damn cute and dramatic when he got high on me. "How was your day off?"

"You trying to be funny?" I ducked under his arm, only to be caught by him gripping my hips and holding me in place against him.

"I don't feel bad for sending you home, J. You were late, and you've been snappy lately. You needed a day."

"Yeah, okay," I muttered and stepped back. "I'm sure that was the reason."

"What's that supposed to mean?" He closed the space between us. "Huh?"

Towering over me, he stared down at me, his eyes roaming my serious expression as his scowl softened. He remained soft, gentle and patient with me, even when his temper was enraged.

Even when he wasn't in the best mood.

Even when he wasn't feeling me or something I'd said.

"It means you had a point to prove when you sent me home in front of everyone. Your boss was watching from across the room and you put on a show."

Quinton brushed his hand down his face and shook his head. "Real talk?" he asked.

I shrugged and cocked my head to the side.

"Because my boss was watching, I had to send you home. You think I wanted to make that move, J? Just because we fuck on the regular doesn't mean I can accommodate your needs during business hours."

"Oh yeah? You had no problem fucking me senseless in the custodial closet before I left." I poked his chest. "I'm tired of arguing about work with you. You clearly never get where I'm coming from."

We'd mixed business with overwhelming plea-sure. I knew this could happen and proceeded to build a relationship with him anyway. Quinton and I never said we were together. Nothing between us was confirmed. However, we played the part, we shared the same immense feelings for each other, and we didn't know how to keep our hands off of each other.

According to him, we were a thing, but if you'd asked me, I wish we never did it. I was only grateful we had. He was an experience I wouldn't have traded for anything in the world.

"You've clearly never fucked with a real nigga before," he said, heading for the front door.

Laughing to myself, I watched him reach for the doorknob. What a dramatic ass exit! But he was right. I hadn't. Far as I knew, Quinton didn't lie or hold anything back to salvage my feelings. I had no reason to doubt him, but hey! Lately, I'd been doubting everything going on in my life.

"Quinton." I sighed. "Wait." I caught up with him and placed my hand on top of his, stopping him from turning the doorknob. "I didn't mean to pick a fight. I know you have a job to do. It's just..." I paused and looked down, struggling to find the right words to describe what was going on inside of my head.

"It's just what?" He lifted my head with a finger. "Tell me something, J. Anything. You've been acting out on me. One day you want me and the next day you look at me like I'm a stranger to you."

"I'm sorry," I whispered.

"I don't want you to be sorry. I want you to be certain about us."

"Quinton." Tears welled in my eyes as I swallowed hard. My emotions always spazzed out at the wrong time.

"Are you certain about us? Is this going somewhere? Or are things between us just a game to you?"

"Can we talk about this tomorrow?" I blinked back tears while avoiding his menacing stare.

Quinton chuckled, followed by a faint scoff. "Yeah." His deep voice emitted low and a bit defeated. "Yeah, sure." He kissed my forehead, then turned away from me. "I'll catch you tomorrow."

"Wh-what? You're not staying over tonight? I baked peanut butter cookies. Your favorite," I whispered and then cringed immediately after I said it. After acting iffy with him for over a week, I couldn't believe I was trying to bribe him with soft-baked, peanut butter cookies.

"Another time," he said, turning the doorknob to leave. "Lock up behind me."

I did as he said, then slid onto the floor with my back against the door. I couldn't deny pushing him away, all because he'd come into my world and changed my perspective on love and what I wanted out of life.

Before encountering him, I was content and satisfied with my life. I was alone every night, but that was okay. Some months I lived paycheck to paycheck, but that was okay, too. I knew how to take care of myself; I knew how to survive.

Then, Quinton's genuine intentions made me believe in love again. He caressed my body with care and tended to my mind with patience. He challenged me to want more by reminding me of what I was good at. Something as simple as baking his favorite cookies from scratch brought on compliments and deep conversations about how far I could take my skill.

Falling in love with Quinton Finch terrified me. But it was too late, I was falling —falling from the tallest building in the world with a never-ending drop point.

THE NEXT MORNING, I ran like I was being chased down the road. On the treadmill in the corner of my office, I ran hard like my life depended on it. The television mounted to the wall displayed a random romantic comedy movie I'd selected on Netflix. Though the television was muted, the subtitles populated on the bottom of the screen.

I ran like I was running out of time to get a good work out in. Truth was, I didn't have anywhere to be. Tuesday's and Wednesday's were considered my weekends. Being sent home on Monday turned my time off into a mini vacation, and without any new baking orders to fulfill from my website, I was idle until I found something else to occupy my time.

Every time my thoughts rounded back to Quinton, I upped the pace and struggled to keep up with the new setting. The faster I ran, the more his absence impacted me. As a woman who believed anything was possible, escaping my feelings for him challenged my belief.

Stopping the treadmill, I hopped off and laid on the carpet while trying to catch my breath. As I stared up at the ceiling, I wondered if Louisville's weather was treating the peppers and lilies in my flower bed out front right. I hoped the sun produced the nutrients they needed.

On my back, I scooted toward my desk at the sound of a text alert on my phone. My best friend, Molli, had her own signature text and call alert—a horn sound that expressed how abrupt and loud she usually was.

"Well, hello to my best friend in the whole entire world," I snatched my phone and said, answering her just in time. I'd already missed three previous calls from her. If it happened again, she would've shown up at my door to check on me before proceeding to curse me out.

"Mhm," she hummed, and I just knew she was rolling her eyes, too. "Check your text messages. I sent you something."

Placing her on speakerphone, I transitioned to our text thread. I read the open mic poetry flyer, then nodded like she could see me. The theme was romance.

"Of course, I'll be there to support you. You should perform that poem I read over last month for you. It was amazing," I said.

"Thank you, friend. I loved it, too. But I can't do that. I wish I could because it's relevant to my budding love life right now, but I already put the piece in my upcoming novel. Can't have it tied to my real name."

Molli Hill was one of the greatest writers I had the pleasure of knowing. Passionate, too. Three years ago, we met at a popular poetry club downtown,

Louisville Kentucky. I approached her to compliment her set, and after a quick conversation about our love for the art, she talked me into getting on stage and facing my fears. Though I almost bombed during my performance and never got back on stage after that, it felt good to do it. Later that night, I scratched it off my bucket list with a smile.

As for our greeting, it transpired into a friendship of a lifetime. Molli was my girl, and a constant inspiration to me. Her successful writing career motivated me to do what I loved. Her readers recognized her storytelling under the popular pen name, M. Hill, so she had to be careful not to completely out herself.

"Do you have another piece up your sleeve?" I asked.

"Not quite."

"Do you want me to help you expand what you have in mind?"

"Jana, you aren't slow or dense, girl. I know you see where this is going. You haven't performed in years."

"Oh no." I laughed to myself, covering my mouth before I turned hysterical over the thought. "I thought we moved on from this."

"Oh, c'mon. It'll be good for you, and its National Poetry Month. Besides, performing in front of a group of your peers is liberating. I know you remember how that feels. You were hype after you stepped off that stage three years ago."

"Molli, I stammered through my whole poem. I was hype about it being over."

Her hard laughter made me roll my eyes. Performing on a stage in front of an audience was different than performing on a live video recording. My YouTube viewers couldn't see my face, and I was in the privacy of my own home. Easy peasy.

"Glad I amuse you."

"I didn't even finish my piece when I got on that stage for the first time. I said a few lines and froze. My sisters rescued me and threatened everyone to clap for me anyway."

"No way." I gasped, struggling to hold back a loud cackle.

"If only I had a time machine..." She paused and then sighed. "But you! You actually finished, girl. And that's all that matters. Who cares that you stammered a few times? What matters is, you got through it and everyone cheered because your poem was powerful."

"Stop trying to talk me into this shit." I groaned.

"Is it working?"

"Unfortunately."

"Woot woot," she cheered, and I held my phone away from my ear until she finished. "I'll pick you up at seven. And I'll check in with you later, I have a brunch date."

"With Grayson? Ooo. Y'all are getting serious, huh?" I teased. "Wait. Why can't I just meet you there tonight?"

Molli kissed her teeth. "You think I trust you to show up on your own? Girl please!" she said, then disconnected our call.

Standing from the floor, I dug my toes in the fluffy, beige carpet and sighed. It was going to be a long day of creating while in my feelings, especially because I missed Quinton like I hadn't seen him in days.

Before I ditched my iPhone to focus on writing a fresh piece for tonight's event, I forwarded him the flyer Molli had sent me, along with a short message:

If you're up for an apology, meet me there at eight.

CHAPTER 2

"NEED I remind you that we're going to a poetry event?" Molli looked me up and down when I answered the door. Her light brown eyes bounced over me as she judged every inch of my V-neck, navy blue romper. It hugged my waist and stopped at the middle of my ample thighs. The long sleeves on it stopped right at the end of my wrists, leaving plenty room for my charm bracelets to shine.

"Do you have a hot date afterward or something?" she asked, side-eying my black, six-inch pumps. Her T-shirt, jean shorts and sandal combo made me feel a little overdressed. Then again, she wasn't the one performing tonight.

I shrugged. "Maybe," I mumbled, then moved aside to look in the full-length mirror on the wall beside the front door. "I invited Quinton," I said, leaving out the high possibility of him not showing out.

Quinton hadn't texted me back and I knew it wasn't because he was at work. He always responded to my texts promptly. It was clear to me that he was upset with me, and I couldn't deny his right to be. In the midst of trying to figure out my purpose in life, I was running from my true feelings for him, and treating him like he was disposable to me in the process.

"You invited your sex toy?" Her eyes widened as she walked in and closed the door behind her. "Mm mm mm." She folded her arms across her chest and shook her head. "I told you this would happen."

"You did," I confirmed while applying a final coat of my favorite plum lip gloss. What started out as risky sex with my boss transpired into something a lot deeper. Molli said I would lose control of the situation if it went on for too long, and she was right. Sex with him was a mind-blowing experience. However, his beautiful mind, intelligence, gentleness, and overall being was too captivating to quit.

"You love that man, don't you?" she asked, snapping me out of my daze in the mirror. I'd gotten lost

in my own eyes and flustered over my thoughts
of him.

"It's complicated."

"Try me." She put her hand on her hip, snapping her neck for emphasis. We looked into each
other's eyes and burst into laughter. Molli had
spotted her own boy toy, Grayson, in a restaurant he
partly owned. Within an hour of encountering him,
she'd found herself in his office, having her breath
kissed away by him. That was one helluva greeting,
and they hadn't slowed down to fully comprehend
what was going on between them yet. If anyone
understood falling in love beyond their control, it
was her.

"I know I love him, Mol, but I don't know what
comes after that. I don't know how to tell him. I don't
know how we'll move forward once he knows I—" I
swallowed hard, then rolled my eyes at how dramatic
my feelings were for him. It was disgusting how
mushy he made me feel inside.

Beautifully disgusting.

"You have a serious problem, you know that?"
Looping her arm in mine, she turned us to face the
mirror as she rested her head on my arm. In six-inch
pumps, I'd finally caught up to her long legs.
Through the mirror, she looked into my eyes and

flashed a faint smile. "You love being in control of everything," she said. "Every. Little. Thing."

"I feel safe that way." I challenged her with a glare that quickly diverted into a smile.

"It's okay to go with the flow sometimes. To lay back and relax without overthinking every aspect of your life. To take trusting God and the universe to a new level and just let things be."

"I can't believe this advice is coming from you. We're just alike in that sense."

"Yeah, but there's levels to this, and you have surpassed mine, girlfriend. You take this shit to a whole new—"

"I get it." I rolled my eyes and dropped my head. My curls fell in front of me.

"Aht Aht! Crown up," she chirped.

Molli, who wasn't that great at showing her emotions or being sentimental, wrapped her arms around me and squeezed me tightly.

"Let's go." She rubbed my back. "And leave it all on the stage tonight."

"You're performing too?"

"Nope." She pulled me toward the door as I snatched my purse from the stand next to it. "You're performing for us."

Just like that, and with an intense roll of my eyes,

we were out of the door, then inside of her car to start our night.

Due to Molli's clout at the Stardust Lounge, we bypassed a long line of patrons waiting to get in. We approached a giant, over-the-top muscular bouncer who looked angry until Molli spoke to him. At the sight of her, his face softened. Towering over her, he looked down at her, admiring her until he couldn't help but smirk. He unfolded his arms and removed his game face to show her respect. There was a deep connection between them that I would have to remember to ask her about later on.

"Have a good time." He nodded for us to head inside. That was the only dialogue between them. Their eyes spoke for them, exposing their love and respect for one another. It was obvious to me that something had gone on between them before.

"What was that?" I spoke closely to her ear as we entered the lounge.

On the stage across the room, the band performed a peaceful jazz tune. The pianist hummed softly in the mic propped up before him.

Swaying from side to side to their melody was inevitable for anyone who entered the lounge.

"Nothing. He's an old friend of mine." She waved me off and led us to the bar.

"I bet," I mumbled behind her, and she looked over her shoulder with a sly smirk on her face.

"They have a new frozen drink called Pink Panties. It's really good but it'll sneak up on you, so drink slow. It has a lot of vodka in it."

I simply nodded as she opened a tab and ordered for us. I'd discovered the Pink Panty drink on Pinterest months ago and made it for myself a few times. Since then, I'd become a little *too* familiar with it. Deeming it delicious would've been an understatement.

While waiting for my drink, I scanned the neon, luminous bar, then looked back at the crowd piling inside. Groups of three and four patrons were taking seats around oval tables in front of the stage. Some were even pushing tables together with other groups to form a crowd of their own. I smiled at all the glowing melanin taking over the room. I thought I would be too nervous to follow through on performing, but surprisingly, I felt right at home. It was the same feeling that overwhelmed me the first time I visited the dim, homey lounge, except I wasn't scared this time around.

By the time I was called to the stage, I was ready. Of course, Molli had jumped the gun and put my name at the top of the list. She wouldn't have been her if she didn't take control and make sure I followed through on my word.

"Jana Monae," the announcer repeated. He squinted his eyes and scanned the crowd for a sign of someone approaching. I scanned the crowd, too. Quinton was missing and my heart was aching.

"She's coming!" Molli shouted as I downed the rest of my frozen drink. A tormenting brain freeze took my attention away from my shattering heart. My watch stated that it was five minutes until eight p.m. Aside from my father, Quinton was the most punctual man I knew. If he was going to be late, he just wouldn't show up at all.

"Hey wait." Molli threw her arms around my neck and squealed. "You're going to kill it up there. Don't forget to speak from your heart. I love you, girl."

"Love you too, friend." I escaped her strong hold and stumbled back a bit. Whenever Molli drank, her strength increased, and her emotions rushed to the forefront.

My heart may have been aching, but I strutted to the stage anyhow. A few whistles welcomed me to the stage, and I smiled when I got up there and noticed they were mostly from other women out in the crowd, along with my best friend's cheers.

"Good evening, everyone. How y'all feeling?" I asked as I adjusted the height of the mic.

Everyone in attendance shouted, "Good," in unison, and that made me smile again. No wonder Molli loved this place. The aesthetic and vibe of it was unmatched. It was a feel-good establishment meant for creatives and those who loved to be surrounded by them.

I was going to start my performance off by telling the crowd to be patient with me if I stumbled over my words, but I decided against it. Taking a deep breath, I closed my eyes and prayed for God to guide me as I free-styled a piece I'd only thought about writing. When I tried to put the pen to a fresh notepad, I struggled to write anything down. I spent more time getting dressed than figuring out what I was going to perform.

Time was up!

I opened my eyes to all eyes on me.

"I call this, *When I Look at You,*" I whispered into the mic.

"Yasss," Molli cheered from the bar. I looked over to smile at her, then spotted *him*. Quinton was in attendance, standing in the back corner of the lounge, staring directly at me.

It was a struggle, but I stripped my eyes away from him and nodded at the band behind me to follow my lead. I loved reciting my poetry with a soft melody in the background. After clearing my throat, I blushed at the thought of Quinton and then started.

"When I look at you, it's like I'm looking at a dream come true.

My dream come true.

My happily ever after and until the end of time.

The guy who is willing to risk it all and be all mine,

To have to myself, a man who I finally do not have to share with anyone else."

I paused to take another deep breath. I was exposing my true feelings for him, and he was in the building, solely focused on me.

"When I look at you, I see your eyes telling me that you only want me,

I see strength, perseverance, protection, provider and all things in between.

Looking at you, shows just how much love and

care you have for me. For us. Your eyes reveal just how much you want us to work."

The band behind me played so well that I couldn't help my body from swaying from side to side.

"How dare you come into my life and make feel like this?" I giggled to myself, then turned serious again.

"When I look at you, I feel as if I am on top of the world,

The way you look at me reveals that you think I am the most beautiful girl.

That I am all you want and all you will ever need.

It's like looking at my best friend and imperfectly perfect man all wrapped into one.

I see so many date nights, vacations, and all-around fun.

Looking at you, is like looking at the moon and stars,

Like laying on the beach watching the sunrise.

When I look at you, I see my happy place,

I see all the love you have for me written all over your face.

I see a manly, man,

One of confidence and intelligence.

A black king of poise and prestige.

I see the guy who I want to be all for me!

The one I need.

The one who is doing a damn good job at making and keeping me happy."

I took a short break from speaking to feel the rhythm of the beautiful melody behind me.

"Quinton, when I look at you, I see you for you, flaws and all, all of you,

It's like I'm looking at a dream come true.

My dream come true."

As my performance ended and snaps and cheers erupted from the crowd, I ran off stage to escape inside of the nearest restroom. With no success, I bumped into his hard chest. I hadn't meant to incorporate Quinton's name into my poem, it just happened that way. It flowed like that because every word was meant for him.

"Where are you going?" He embraced me warmly in his arms.

"With you," I whispered, staring up into his eyes.

From the corner of my eye, I saw Molli's high-laced sandal in the air. She was leaning against a man at the bar, flirting with one of her feet up. I broke my intense staring contest with Quinton to check if she was drunk off her ass and flirting with a stranger. But the guy she was all up on was no stranger. I recognized the one and only, Grayson, from the adorable photos she'd recently sent me of them.

Suddenly, our eyes met, and we smiled and nodded at each other. We both knew we were going home with the men we loved.

"Quinton," I whispered, letting the strong drink I'd swigged guide my emotions. "I think I might love you."

"Okay new sectional," I teased him as I walked around his living room. "I see you."

We usually resorted to my place to spend time together or make love until we were physically spent. However, I loved the far and few times we spent at his condo. Each visit taught me more about him. I admired his cleanness and organization. I recognized OCD when I saw it and he had a healthy case of it. It sometimes seemed like I was in the apartment of a fifty-year-old man instead of a thirty-one-year-old stud, but I liked his vintage, laid-back style.

Quinton was not only a man of great taste, he moved with precision and he paid great attention to detail. He noticed and sometimes pointed out the smallest things about me.

"You fuck with it?" He slapped my ass, then squeezed it. "Had it delivered yesterday. You down for breaking it in?"

I nodded. "It looks nice and sturdy, too." The black fabric sectional set also looked inviting. I plopped down onto the middle of it, then propped my feet on the padded stool in front of it. But not before kicking my heels off.

Wiggling my toes, I admired my baby blue gel pedicure. They matched my nails and both sets looked foreign to me against my light brown skin. My nail color was preferably black, but during any emotional crisis, I had the nerve to switch things up.

Getting comfortable next to me, Quinton moved my feet onto his lap. Both of his large hands massaged my feet at once, causing my eyes to roll to the back of my head.

"Quinton," I moaned.

"Damn, woman. That's how you sound when I'm rubbing that—"

"Sir." I lifted my head and glared at him. It wasn't long before a wide smile revealed my high cheekbones and ruined my poker face. "Do you know how to behave?"

"Around you? Hardly." Smirking, he licked his lips. He massaged my feet with love, but that was no shocker. His overall touch was love. His dark brown skin glistened like silk.

I stared into his handsome face and wondered how he did it. At work, Quinton was always upbeat, happy and positive. Even when he had to apply pressure and discipline someone under him, he remained professional and kept a smile on his face at all times. When we were together, he was smooth, charming and focused on me. No matter how much I pushed him away or gave him whiplash with my constant back and forth, he never stopped being persistent with proving his intentions.

Damn, I was exhausted for him.

"How are you, Quinton?"

Looking up from my feet, he said, "I'm straight." He only answered in two ways whenever I asked him that—*straight or good*.

"Is everything okay?" I removed my feet from his lap, replacing them with my ass.

"Careful with all that," he quipped.

"Are your grandparents okay?" I asked. Quinton worked hard to take care of his grandparents. Him and his younger sister were raised by them, and they were all they'd even known. They went out of their way to make sure their grandparents were happily retired.

"Yeah, they're good. Kiara is good, too. Ever since she popped up and ran into you leaving that morning, she's asked about you every day."

"She looked like she wanted to beat me up."

Quinton chuckled. "Nah. That's just her face. She's a spoiled, mean brat and she's overprotective of me. She called you beautiful, though, and I agreed."

"You better had." I punched his arm. "She's beautiful, too. Those golden eyes must run in the family."

"That's what my grandmother says." He squeezed my hip, but it wasn't a regular squeeze. It was an apprehensive one—a soft squeeze that alarmed me something was up. "Davidson promoted me to Operations Manager."

"No way!" I gasped, then cheered. "About freaking time! You deserve that position. What did he say?"

"That's exactly what he said, that I deserve it. I challenged him to put his money where his mouth is, and he accepted my salary request."

Gently, I bounced up and down on his lap, squealing as I wrapped my arms around his neck. "I'm happy for you."

"I know," he said. "Would've been nice to experience this excitement from you on the day it happened."

My stomach dropped to my ass and my mouth followed suit. My eyebrows crinkled and then my thoughts drifted back to the last night we saw each other.

"Quinton." I kissed my teeth and shook my head at myself. "I'm—"

"I can't play these mind games with you anymore, J. Shit started out as out as a thrill for me, but now I'm tired. Chasing you has worn me out."

"Oh," I whispered, then removed myself from his lap. On the cushion next to him, I avoided his eyes. They bounced around the boring room until there was nothing left to do but face him. "I see."

"No, you don't," he grumbled, then chuckled. "Check me, your words tonight were beautiful, but will there be any actions behind them? Will you show me you want me instead of pushing me away? Are you willing to grow with me despite your fears? Do you see a future with me?"

When did he become a damn poet?

"I don't think I might love you, Jana. I know I do." My breathing hitched as he pulled me back onto his lap. "I haven't told you because I knew you couldn't handle it."

"I can handle it," I interjected.

"You're not ready for what we could be."

Leaping from his lap, I stood in front of him and shook my head. "That's not it."

"Open your mouth and tell me what it is." He followed my lead, standing to approach me. "Without riddles, games, or hesitation. Tell me," he demanded. "Do you even know what it is?"

"I'm in love with you and it scares the fuck out of me. Not because I've been hurt before or fear this will end badly. But because no man has ever made me feel the way you make me feel. Because you make me feel like I'm everything you've ever wanted. Yet, I still want to be more for you. *Do* more for you." Tears welled in my eyes as I sucked in a breath, then exhaled deeply. "My God. No one told me that love overwhelms you with emotions like this. What the fuck is this?" I flailed my arms in the air.

"Believe me. You aren't in this alone." Quinton grabbed my arms before I let them drop defeatedly. Snatching me into him, he leaned down and placed a soft kiss on my collarbone.

"Take this off." He fingered my sleeve. "And join me in the shower in five minutes." Before he left me in his living room with my juices tricking down my thighs, he grabbed my neck and kissed the side of my lips. "Hurry up," he mumbled against them. His full lips overshadowed mine.

I wondered if he realized his effortless impact on me. Truth be told, he could get whatever he wanted out of me if he played his cards right. From where I stood, he surely knew how to play 'em.

During a random conversation in each other's arms one night, we agreed that shower sex was trash, so I knew he wasn't after that in this moment.

Quinton had this fascination with pampering me, caressing my body and bathing me whenever the chance presented itself. Regardless of it being beyond my understanding, he knew what his touch did to me.

Dropping my romper to my ankles, I cleared my throat and called behind him, "I'll be right there."

CHAPTER 3

"I'm leaving," he mumbled in my ear, then buried his head in my hair and inhaled me.

I groaned and wrapped my arms around his neck. "Already?"

After a beautiful night of reassurance and cuddling, I wasn't ready for him to depart from me just yet. I deserved more of his undivided attention.

He chuckled as I pulled him fully down onto the bed with me. "C'mon, J. You gon' wrinkle my suit."

"Look at you. Dressing in suits and shit now. You used to wear joggers and Jordan's to work every day."

"I still plan on it. The clients will be there today. They sent an email out for everyone to dress professionally."

"In that case, I'm glad I'm off," I said, rolling my eyes.

If masculinity and cinnamon came together to build a brand, Quinton would be the face of it. He smelled too good for me to release him from my tight embrace.

"How'd you sleep?" he asked, settling next to me.

"Like a baby." I snuggled closely to him and laid my head on his hard chest. I couldn't resist looking up at his handsome face and smiling.

I may have been scared of my feelings for him, but I wasn't opposed to having them...

Experiencing them...

Blissfully drowning in them.

"That full body massage did me a lot of good."

"Good." He kissed my forehead, then flipped me onto my stomach. I yelped from how fast we transitioned. His warm hands palmed my ass and calmed me down. I cooed from the therapeutic pressure of him squeezing my ass. With no time to object, he spread my ass cheeks and rubbed my clit from the back. I wouldn't have stopped him if I could. His touch was addicting.

"Can I ask you something?" He kissed my back, leading down to the top of my ass where he placed a final kiss. In his presence, I enjoyed being naked, bare and exposed in every way possible.

"Y-yes," I managed to answer through soft moans.

"What do you desire to do?" he asked. His full lips graced the side of my neck, then brushed against my ear. "You're great at so many things. When you actually show up to work and get down to business, you're the best agent in the building." He chuckled. "But you're a creator, J. An artist. What do you plan to do with those skills?"

Flipping over to face him, I spread my legs for him to lie between them.

While staring into his golden-brown eyes, I said, "I don't want to be limited. I want to bake, sing and write."

"*Sing?*" He towered over me like he was doing push-ups. His bright orbs widened, and I snickered.

"I know my day job is necessary. My savings account is pretty nice, but I still need my day job. Right now, it's my foundation. Those thirteen dollars an hour fund my dreams and buys all the material and equipment I need to do what I love in my spare time." Taking a break from his intense gaze, I closed my eyes and took a deep breath. When I opened them again, he was still focused on me like his life depended on it.

"It's an easy job for me with decent pay," I continued. "I don't mean to complain while I'm there or give my fine ass boss a hard time." I side-eyed him, then blushed. "It's just... all I can think about is baking or doing something I love while I'm there. Eight to ten hours a day with only two days of free time can be overwhelming. Sometimes I feel like that shit is taking over my life."

"I understand," he said.

"Do you?"

"What? You think because I love what I do that I don't understand? I've worked jobs I wasn't feeling and felt the same way you do. I get it. With this job, I went back to school and got my business degree. The company paid for it because of how long I've worked there. I almost got comfortable answering phones until I made a move to move up in the company," he explained. "I get it. You just want to do what you love at the end of the day. Without having to press pause and work for someone else who won't get you where you're trying to go."

As he spoke, I watched his lips.

Damnit, why was it so hard to act civilized around him?

My thoughts weren't this disgusting until I encountered him. He brought it out of me. Emotionally, I was wide open for him and it made me want to be sexually available for him to have me all day, every day.

"You'll get there, and I want to help you figure it out," he said, and that caught my undivided attention. No one I'd ever dated had said anything like that to me before. Tears welled in my eyes, so I closed them.

"There's something else I want," I whispered. He relaxed his body onto mine, and I welcomed the pressure of his six-five, two-hundred and thirty-pound muscled frame on top of me.

"Tell me."

"I want to flourish as a lover, without fear or overthinking the future. I want to love you to the best of my ability, without thinking there should be a timeframe to our progression or where we're separately headed," I said. "Quinton, when it comes to you, I've realized that I just want to love you, and I'm sorry for how I've complicated things between us."

"I think I'll work from home today," he said, then kissed my bottom lip. I giggled and locked my legs around his waist as he slung his suit jacket across his bedroom floor.

"All of it." I nodded. "Take it all off."

I snatched at his shirt as he kicked off his pants. Once we were skin to skin, my heart raced and the butterflies in my stomach followed suit. His hard dick brushed against my sensitive clit and I almost had an orgasm on impact.

"I wasn't going to give up on you," he confessed, and the tears that'd welled in my eyes fell down my cheeks. Quinton kissed them away. He kissed over my cheeks, spoiling me with gentle pecks until a loud gasp emitted from me. My back arched, then slowly unraveled as he instructed me to relax. His dick filled me up, threatening my tightness each time he slowly stroked inside of me.

"Oh... my..." It wasn't possible to get used to his commendable size. No matter how much I tried to take it for him, I wound up trying to escape and run up the headboard. Eventually, I bossed up and handled the immense pleasure and pain combination like the good, naughty princess he whispered in my ear and called me.

"You gon' take this dick for me?" His deep, sultry voice took me over the edge. Unable to speak, I whimpered and nodded.

He pushed so deeply every time he was inside of me that I just knew our souls were tied. If I wasn't on birth control, I would've borne his children without an objection. Little did he know, I'd dreamed of having a family with him. Not only was loving him easy, it was easy envisioning a future with him.

"I forgive you, beautiful. I'm not going anywhere," he reassured in my ear.

I JUMPED up and down on Quinton's super king-sized bed, bouncing high on the memory foam mattress. While working from his iPad, he griped about emails and people not doing their jobs properly. Something told me he was going to be stricter and more prone to micromanage with his new position.

His attention was what I was after. After jumping high for five minutes and wearing myself out, I finally got it. Quinton put his iPad on the nightstand, then wrapped his hand around my ankle and pulled me down. I landed on my back and then he pulled me into his arms.

"My nieces are turning five soon," I randomly blurted.

"The trips," he said, smirking. That's what he referred to them as. Their personalities blew me away sometimes. Whenever I told him funny stories about my nieces, I reminded him that they were all a trip. It amused me that his nickname for them was also short for triplets. "What are we getting them?" he asked. He'd never met them, just like he'd never met my sister and brother, or my parents. That didn't stop him from frequently asking how my family were doing. From how much I rambled about them, he probably felt he knew them already.

"I have my eye on this big, pink dollhouse that I think they'll love. They're really into dolls right now." I eyed my phone that was across the room, on top of the dresser. I wanted to show him pictures of the dollhouse that I'd saved in my phone months ago but relaxing in his arms felt too good to disturb. "Take my word for it." I exhaled deeply as he ran his fingers through my curls. "It's super cute."

How much is it?"

"No," I said, already knowing where his question was headed. "Thank you for always trying to front the bill, but I'm okay."

"What do you have against me fronting the bill?"

"You do a lot for me already. What more can I do for you?"

Quinton turned me to face him, and I straddled his lap. Resting my head on his shoulder, I stared at his beard and felt the moisture between my thighs increase.

"You're more than enough."

"I want you to meet my family," I said, tracing over the hairs on his chest. "And I want to meet yours, but only when the time is right. I've brought a few unworthy people around my family," I admitted, then shuddered at the thought.

I'd introduced a few men to my mother and sister who didn't deserve to even shake their hands. As far as my father and brother were concerned, they weren't impressed or fond of any of them, anyway.

My mother and sister were the ones who welcomed people into our circle with open arms. I promised myself I would be more careful with who I brought around my family moving forward. Not to mention, Mom didn't know how to move on. Once she met someone new, she asked how they were doing frequently, or inquired when was the last time I'd spoken to or saw them. I respected and admired her big heart, but I wished she didn't ask me about people who fucked me over.

"That doesn't mean I don't think you're worthy, because I do. You're worthy, Quinton," I whispered in his ear, then paused to kiss his enticing lips. "My family means a lot to me. You're special to me, but I want to be careful with that part of us. We're just getting started and—"

"Aye." He lifted my head before I could officially drop it. "Tell me what you want and stand on that shit. You don't have to drive yourself crazy explaining why you feel the way you do. My family means a lot to me, too. We're here," he said, pointing from his eyes with two fingers to mine. His dark brown skin glowed against my tan complexion as I held him closely.

"But eventually you'll have to show face. I told my grandparents I was dating someone special. My grandma wants you to come over for her legendary peach cobbler soon. She said that'll seal the deal and keep you around."

Quinton didn't anticipate a response. Beneath the heat of my thighs, his dick hardened in his briefs. He pulled it out and spread my legs. The mushroom head of his dick poked my entrance, then inched inside of me slowly like it belonged. I knew it did. My pussy was always ready, dripping, and pulsating for him.

"Come here," he said, requesting my lips. My lips crashed into his at the same time he slapped my ass. "You thought I was going to give up on you," he broke our kiss and said, chuckling a bit.

I thought I was going to end up running him away. To me, that was totally different from him giving up on me. I wouldn't have blamed him for throwing in the towel, and I would've never forgiven myself for weeding him out.

"I thought..." Crashing my lips into his again, I parted his lips with my tongue.

I needed more of him right now. The mere taste of his lips couldn't suffice. Together, we produced a sweet nectar. Quinton was the best I'd ever had, and I hoped I was the same for him.

"Wait, I—"

Interrupted by my own gasp, I threw my head back as he controlled my hips. He guided me up and down his shaft, smirking every time I whimpered.

"What?" He held me in place with one hand, remaining deeply inside of me. "What did you think, Jana?" With a fistful of my curls, he cocked my head slightly to the side and bit my bottom lip. "Humor me."

"I-I don't know what I thought."

"And now?" he asked, then positioned me flat on my stomach. I begged for mercy as his slow strokes persisted, but I didn't want it. I loved when he made me take it for him.

"I'm not letting you go anywhere." I moaned into

the pillow and gripped the silk sheets on his bed. My body trembled as a powerful orgasm ripped through me and blurred my vision. "I love you, Quinton." I panted.

"I love you too, woman," he leaned down and spoke in my ear, kissing my earlobe thereafter. Just when I thought he was done with me, his strokes sped up. "Let me show you."

CHAPTER 4

BEING on time for work awarded me with a close parking spot. I was two rows away from the front entrance of the building which meant the sun wouldn't have a chance to intimidate me before I walked inside. The brazing winds couldn't toss my curls all over my head and ruin my day before it officially started. At least that's what I thought until I got out of my car and started for the door.

During the half-hour drive to work, Doja Cat tunes made me forget how sore my body was. Spending time with Quinton was always fun, sexy and worth it, but I had to escape him last night in order to make it to work this morning. His stamina wouldn't allow me to rest for long, and unlike him, I couldn't work from home.

Limping toward the front entrance, I smiled faintly and waved awkwardly at a few coworkers who were standing across the parking lot gossiping. Pretending I didn't hear one of them ask me if I was okay, I clutched the strap of my crossbody purse tighter and winced as I picked up the pace.

I only had ten minutes to make it to my cubicle and clock in for work. At this rate, it was going to take me every bit of that time to get inside and plop down gently in my seat. My thighs burned, and my ass ached. I loved it when our love-making sessions were rough. When Quinton slapped my ass cheeks, then spread them apart as he pushed deeply inside of me, my soul escaped my body and bowed down to him.

"What's up, pretty girl?" Dru was the first person to greet me when I walked inside of the building. Of course, he was. Sometimes I thought he waited for me to arrive. If he had a chance with me, he would've taken it without a second thought about it. I'd considered it before, until Quinton caught ahold of my attention and showed me why I'd hesitated to take Dru seriously outside of work. He showed me why it'd never worked with anyone else.

"Good morning, Druski," I chimed, returning my

work nickname for him. "How's hell been so far today?"

"Same ol bullshit, different day." He draped his heavy arm around my shoulders and my legs buckled. "People didn't like the movie they chose to watch, so they're calling us for a refund, as if that shit makes sense. The chat is backed up with over a hundred people waiting to get through because our site is down, like always, and agents are complaining and going over their thirty-minute lunch breaks, which backs up the queues even more."

"You're right. Same ol bullshit." I huffed, tripping over my feet.

Dru caught me before I hit the ground. He took his arm from around me and looked me up and down. "You good, pretty girl?"

"Mhm." I nodded, holding back from whimpering over my soreness. "I think I worked out too hard yesterday or something." It wasn't the whole truth, but it wasn't a total lie either. Keeping up with Quinton during our sexual adventures was an epic workout every time.

"Let me help you to your desk," he said, placing his hand at the small of my back.

"I got her," Quinton's deep baritone aired and then his large, familiar hand was at the small of my back. "Do you mind hopping on chats and tending to the escalated cases?" he asked Dru as he pulled me into his side.

"Yeah, no problem man," Dru said. He and Quinton dapped fists and my eyes widened. I didn't understand why my eyes reacted before my mind had a fair chance to comprehend what was happening. Quinton was over everyone in the building now, except one person—his boss. Everyone would be sucking up to him, doing whatever he said, and kissing his ass moving forward, except one person—me. Good thing I was screwing him; he already knew how stubborn I could be.

Dru threw his hand up to say goodbye to me, then headed in the opposite direction. Putting space between Quinton and I, I checked the time on my Apple Watch and walked ahead of him to my section. He was on my heels, so close to me that I felt him clear his throat and shift the tie around his neck.

"You either tell him he's too handsy with you or leave it to me."

"Mr. Finch," I whispered. "Please be professional while we're at work," I joked seriously.

"I'll go let him know right now."

Stopping in my tracks, I whipped around to face him. I looked up at his handsome face, into his dreamy eyes, and almost dropped to my knees to submit to his every beck and will. "I will take care of it," I mumbled. "People are watching us."

"That's not important. I emailed my boss about us after you dipped on me last night. He knows what's up with us and that's all that matters," he said and walked away, leaving me wide-eyed once again, and speechless.

"Damnit," I grumbled to myself as my watch's alarm went off. Though I was inside of the building and only a few feet away from my desk, I was still late.

Good thing I was screwing him.

An hour into my shift, an agent who thought she had a higher position than everyone else on our team, stood and announced an upcoming meeting.

"Yeah, I think we all got the same email, *Karen*," my work neighbor, JoAnn, quipped over her cubicle. I put my annoying customer on hold, then burst into laughter. I didn't know her name, but I was certain Karen wasn't it.

"Real funny, JoAnn the scammer. You, more than anyone, knows my name." She winked at JoAnn, then JoAnn tried to climb over her desk to get to her, but I grabbed ahold of her arm before she pounced.

"Hey. I don't know what that's about but don't let her get to you. She gets off on that."

"Anyway, like I said," Karen, or whatever her name was, continued. "We have an important meeting to attend in twenty-minutes. The email says our team shouldn't take another call after the one we're on, so we make it to the meeting on time."

I glared at her until she sat down and shut up, then turned to JoAnn. "You okay?"

"Yeah, I'll be fine. That bitch thinks she's won because she's fucking my baby's daddy." JoAnn snatched her headset off and tossed it across her desk. "Little does she know, everyone is fucking him, even my gay cousin, David!" Her pale cheeks turned red as she stormed away from her desk in the direction of the bathrooms. I felt the pain in her voice and knew she was headed for an empty stall to cry in.

"Not her gay husband, David," Charlene, my other work neighbor who sat to the opposite side of me, whispered and snickered.

I cleared my throat, then unmuted my phone before taking my customer off hold. "Mr., Richardson? Are you there?" I repositioned the long, skinny mic of my headset by my lips as he came back onto the line. "Great. Thank you for holding. Sorry about that long hold time. I've gone ahead and put a credit on your account for the amount of those two movie tickets. The amount is twenty-two dollars and thirty-six cents. It doesn't expire and you can use it at any time."

"What do I do? Just go on there like usual?" His thick, country accent made me want to laugh. It reminded me of Goofy from *A Goofy Movie*.

"Yes, that's correct. When you get to the checkout page, the credit will automatically apply to the new order's amount."

"Okay. Thank you for your help, ma'am."

"No problem, Mr. Richardson. In the meantime, I want to remind you that you have up until the very minute of your showing to request a credit or refund on the Fandango app. I've given you a courtesy credit, but in the future, refunds and exchanges cannot be processed on your end or mine after the showtime has started."

"Well, that's the dumbest shit I've ever heard. If I didn't see the movie, why can't I get a refund or exchange? A buddy of mine told me y'all were robbing people of their money. Doesn't look like I'll be using y'all anymore."

"Is there anything else I can—" A beeping sound blared in my ear, indicating that he'd hung up on me.

"Damn." I shook my head. "And I thought we were on the same page."

"No way you thought that," Charlene's nosy ass said. She feasted on a bag of chips as she leaned back in her chair, staring at me while I worked. Right after Karen announced the meeting, she'd hung up on her customer, pretending she had phone troubles, and used the upcoming meeting as an opportunity to do nothing.

Looking around the expansive, one story building, I tried to wrap my mind around the thousands of agents who worked in one building. We were spread out in large sections, separated by teams and different departments within the company. Depending on how long you'd work there, the white, orange and blue walls that matched the Fandango logo got tiresome of seeing and being between after a while.

I looked toward the women's bathroom for a sign of JoAnn. We usually sat together in meetings and whispered our complaints to each other. Walking in the direction of the bathrooms to find her, I reached the long, narrow hallway of them and was snatched in the opposite direction. Trapped inside of a dark, stuffy storage closet, my mouth was covered by his before I could react.

"Mind your business," Quinton broke our kiss and said.

"Hey! Be careful with me, I'm already sore because of you. And how'd you—"

"Word travels fast around here, especially when people go back and forth on the production floor. I know that's ya' lil homegirl."

If the closet wasn't pitch black, he would've witnessed how hard I rolled my eyes at that.

"If only you knew how many unauthorized work group chats are floating around on our server. We have access to all of them. I'm glad you aren't apart of any of them, so continue minding your business. Don't get involved in anything."

"I just wanted to check on her and see if she's okay," I explained, then exhaled deeply as he kissed my neck. "Were you watching me or something?"

I'd wondered if he could see me from his new office, wherever that was. I supposed I'd already gotten my answer.

"I haven't been able to stop watching you since you told me you loved me."

I accidentally smashed my lips into his chin, then found his full, delicious lips. Quinton held me in his arms, gently caressing my body as I uncontrollably released soft moans.

"I have a—" I tried to speak, but he kept interrupting me with passionate, sloppy kisses that I loved. "Mr. Finch." I grabbed his face. "I have a mandatory meeting I have to go to soon."

"I'm in charge of said meeting." He tried to maneuver inside of my black slacks, but I slapped his hand away. "We have to stop meeting like this at work," he said, and I broke out into a fit of giggles.

Every chance he got, he pulled me into a closet, storage unit or vacant office to have a quick fix of me. Sometimes I took extra breaks just to tempt him. He accepted the bait every time.

"Help me, help you."

"Deal." His sensual baritone made me clutch my thighs together. "Right after you come for me."

"Mr. Finch," I whispered harshly to object, but it was too late. His hand had ventured down into my slacks. Two of his fingers pressed against my dripping wet clit, causing me to lean against him as he held me upright. "Quinton," I moaned his name repeatedly as I ground my hips atop his fingers. "Deal," I said, panting and quivering while my juices trickled down his hand.

PILING into the transparent conference room, my team took a seat around the long and wide, boat shaped conference table. They shuffled occasionally, being sure to sit next to the agents they liked, and across from the agents they didn't like so they could glare at them while whispering mean things to their friends.

Call center drama was the worst type of madness. Fandango's call center was the first one I'd worked at and from what I'd experienced, saw and heard overtime, I would never work at another one again.

"Did the email say who was in charge of the meeting?" black tights asked. "Whoever is, they're late." I may not have been that great with names, but I noticed she wore a pair of black tights to work every day.

"Our new operations manager is in charge," Karen said. "With his fine self."

I scrolled through my phone, snickering at my group chat thread with Monae and Monty. They were arguing over each other's opinion about the latest season of Ozark on Netflix and debating about what would probably happen during the next season. Since I'd just started the show, I skimmed their text messages to avoid spoilers, then replied with a few laughing emojis.

Karen's gaze was dead set on me, I felt it. It was filled with envy and confusion. During work hours, she focused on everyone on our team and whatever else was happening around her besides herself. She'd mentioned the way Quinton looked at me before, loudly and in front of everyone. Despite everyone on the team staring at me and anticipating a response, the joke was on her as I acted like she didn't exist.

"You wouldn't happen to know where he is, would you, Jana?" Karen asked with sarcasm taking over her whiny voice.

I looked up and met her eyes, then shrugged. "Nope. But I can remind you where hell is." I smiled.

Underneath the table, JoAnn nudged me and cackled. The rest of the ladies among us burst into laughter as the only three men in the room shook their heads and minded their business. Poor Diana was the eldest person on the team and always fed up with the millennials who surrounded her at work.

"Good afternoon, everyone," Quinton's deep voice entered the conference room before he did. Behind him was our new team lead—an older Latina woman who looked like she didn't play any games when it pertained to her job description. I could tell by the way she overlooked the room and made a few people squirm in their seats.

"This meeting isn't going to be long so pay attention and save your questions for the end. And when we reach the end, please don't try to ask unnecessary questions to prolong our meeting and stay off the phones. That's call avoidance and I know all the tricks."

"Do you now?" Charlene popped an animal cracker in her mouth and laughed.

"I know you hung up on your last customer and claimed you had phone problems," Quinton responded to her. "You may want to tread carefully today, Ms. Williams."

Charlene slumped down in her chair as everyone gasped and looked at each other. Charlene had been hanging up on customers and blaming it on phone problems for years. She'd worked for Fandango's call center before I came along, and she'd taught me how to disconnect mid-sentence and blame it on the phone lines. Regardless of them being aware of her tactics and threatening her frequently, she wasn't going anywhere. For whatever reason, they never fired her. She got away with murder.

"You want to start it off, Ms. Monserrate?" Quinton looked to our new team lead.

"Sure." She blushed. "And I told you to call me Lena."

Quinton nodded for her to take over, then stepped back. Meanwhile, in my head, I'd spoken up to tell her that he would absolutely not be calling her Lena.

Bitch please.

Lena went over things we already knew or should've known. Every week, the rules and guidelines of our job had to be repeated for those who failed to do their job properly. After twenty minutes of pounding proper call flow procedures into our heads, Lena stepped back and nodded for Quinton to take over again.

"Are y'all still with us?" His voice boomed off the walls, waking everyone up as they sat up in their desk chairs. I tried hard to focus on what he was saying, but my eyes couldn't stop dancing over his lips. I squeezed my thighs together and daydreamed of kissing his lips as he spoke.

"We understand that sometimes your fifteen-minute breaks and thirty-minute lunches aren't enough time to grab a bite to eat, then eat without rushing and make it back to work on time."

"Mhm." Karen folded her arms across her chest and nodded. "You got that right."

"Due to the dozens of complaints we've received about this, we are working with local food trucks and restaurants to come up with a plan that will provide everyone delicious options for lunch. Starting next month, you won't have to leave the parking lot to get lunch if you don't want to."

"Will it be free?" a guy who hardly ever spoke, unless he was on a phone call, asked.

"C'mon, man." Quinton chuckled. "You really want me to answer that?"

"You know damn well they aren't paying for everyone in the building's lunch every day." Charlene rolled her eyes.

"Let's be real here." Quinton took control of the room before everyone chimed in with their separate opinions. "Even I have to pay for my own lunch."

"Everyone doesn't have a work husband who buys them lunch every day," Karen said. Cocking her head to one side, she looked directly at me.

"Girl leave me alone before you have to eat through a straw," I said, then smiled faintly at her.

"Ladies," Lena jumped in. "Everyone, please listen up and save your questions and commentary for the end. We only have this conference room for forty-five minutes and we're running out of time."

Quinton cleared his throat, gathering everyone's

undivided attention again. "Last but not least, something that we will be paying for and adding to our company budget are snacks. Sweets to be precise."

"Sweets?" JoAnn whispered, side-eying him.

"Yes. One of your peers, Jana over there." Quinton nodded toward me. He winked at me as everyone shifted in their seats to face me. "Any time there's a potluck, she brings in a lot of sweets and makes sure everyone in the building gets a fair share. If she's willing to do that for us a couple times a week, the management team will make it worth her while, and we're sure it will bring a bit more joy to all agents across the floor."

"It sure would. That girl can bake her ass off. I had to call my grandma and tell her about the lemon cake she brought in during our last potluck," Charlene said.

"Thank you," I looked at her and mouthed, then snapped my neck in Quinton's direction. "I'm sorry... what?"

"Of course, we would compensate you for your time and efforts and we're willing to negotiate if you don't agree with our offer. We only want you to take this on if you can handle it along with your regular work schedule," Quinton explained, and I wanted to leap in his arms, jump his bones and kiss all over his dark brown skin.

My God.

I wanted him more than I'd ever wanted him in this moment.

"Oh my God. Please do it. For us." JoAnn cheered, bouncing up and down in her seat. Everyone started talking among themselves and agreeing that I should do it, but I couldn't focus on their encouragement. My shock was taking over. I didn't know how to respond.

"Settle down everyone," Lena shouted, silencing the room immediately. "Jana, you have a few weeks to decide. All of this would take place next month, along with the food trucks and new lunch options."

I nodded slowly that I understood, but I couldn't peel my eyes away from Quinton and his handsome smirk.

"Our time is up," he said, and everyone groaned and complained. "If you still have questions, comments or concerns, email them to Lena and they will get taken care of."

As we all stood to leave out of the conference room and return to our cubicles, I stared at him a final time and vowed to ride him into oblivion later on.

CHAPTER 5

I WAITED for his signature knock on the door. Like clockwork and almost every night when he got off work, he came over to spend time with me. Time in which we always lost track of and then he ended up spending the night. I wouldn't have had it any other way.

I unlocked the door and stepped back. It wasn't long before he caught on and turned the knob to enter. Quinton locked the door behind him after he entered. He stuffed his hands into his navy-blue slacks and chuckled as we stood across from each other.

"You," I said and shook my head. It was all I could muster right now. The man was something else.

"I don't smell anything baking. The position doesn't have to wait until next month if you're ready to start." He inched toward me, towering over everything in my living room. The closer he got to me, the faster my heart raced. I closed my eyes until he touched me, and when he did, I opened them and smiled.

"You," I repeated, still shaking my head. "Why didn't you give me a heads up?"

"My time with you is my time with you." He shrugged. "Business was discussed where it needed to be discussed at."

"Did you convince them to—"

"Nope. No convincing needed. I reminded them of what else you could bring to the table." He kissed my cheek. "I reminded them that they act like vultures whenever you bring in your baked goods."

"God." I lifted my hand and caressed his smooth, brown cheek. "You're just—"

"In love with you." He grabbed my hand in his and squeezed tightly. "I'm in love with you, Jana, and I'll do anything for you." After kissing the top of my hand, he wrapped his hand around my neck, gently stroking the middle of my neck with his thumb. "Whatever I need to do to support you, I will. Because I want to, and because I believe in you."

"I-I don't know what to say," I whispered.

"Say you'll accept the extra position. It pays well and it allows you to spend more time doing what you love."

"I accept."

"Say you'll let me love you, and that you won't push me away when your love for me overwhelms you."

"I will and I won't."

"Promise me," he whispered in my ear, his hand remaining around my neck.

"I promise," I said, struggling to breathe properly. It wasn't his hand around my neck that affected my breathing. It was him—his willingness to make me happy and his efforts to fight for our togetherness.

Right when he lifted me in his arms and held me up by holding onto my ass cheeks, an alarm sounded from my office. It was the alarm on my iPad, reminding me that I only had twenty-five minutes left before my next live stream on YouTube.

"To my office please," I said, looping my fingers behind his neck. He carried me inside of my office and dropped me on one of the beanbag chairs. "Hey! Be careful with me," I reminded him.

"I know what you can handle, woman," he said, then handed me my blaring iPad. "I'll be back. I'm going to hit the shower." He walked out of the room and I froze.

Our relationship was getting deeper than I imagined it would. Lately, we left extra clothes at each other's places and made ourselves at home. Our progress baffled and swooned me all at once.

I was grateful he didn't invite me to shower with him this time. I wouldn't have been able to deny him, and I would've let my subscribers down. The song I chose to sing this week was one they'd requested, then voted on.

The poll had three options from three amazing artists, and the song that resonated with me the most won. I accepted it as a sign from God.

Preparing to go live, I set up my piano and camera angle, then settled comfortably behind it. I hummed the melody of the tune to get in the right mood, but all I really had to do was consider the tall, dark and handsome man who was currently in the shower of my master bedroom.

Bing!

I'd spent majority of the countdown to showtime overthinking instead of preparing. Without any more time to waste, I straightened my posture and jumped right into it. I wished my viewers well, telling them that I hoped their day turned out to be just as amazing as mine was.

I got through the first verse of Tamia's, *Who Do You Tell* track with ease. By the chorus, I paused playing the piano for a second, then started the chorus over. Despite my eyes being closed, I knew Quinton was standing in the threshold watching me. I could sense that beautiful man at any time, and also, his sweet, masculine scent had gotten really familiar to me.

"Who do you tell when you love someone? Hoping that someone's in love with you. Who do you tell when you love someone? I think I might as well tell you."

It took a while, but eventually, I got through the song, thanked my viewers, then ended the live and stood immediately. I was so nervous to have sung in front of him that I was acting erratically.

"I..."

Nothing.

I tried to find something to say and got nothing.

"That's cute," he said. "All that shit you talk, and you got the nerve to be shy. Come here."

I rushed into his embrace and laid my head against his bare chest.

"Your voice, like everything else about you, is beautiful. Wow." He cupped my face and gazed into my eyes.

"Thank you," I whispered and turned my head to inhale the side of his hand. His skin was naturally soft, but it was especially soft after a shower.

"You trying to sing me another song? I have a special request."

"Oh yeah? What's that?" I asked, already giggling in preparation for him to say something corny and disgusting. I loved that type of shit from him. He could do no wrong.

"My name while you ride this dick." He threw me over his shoulder like a rag doll and carried me to our bedroom. Oh boy were we at our best when we were slutting each other out.

Quinton tossed me onto the bed and snatched his towel from his waist. Smiling from ear to ear, I licked my lips and watched his every move as he moved toward me. His dick was hard and intimidating but so fucking gorgeous that I couldn't help but want it.

Need it.

Lifting my oversized T-shirt to my waist, I exposed that I was bare underneath it. An hour before he arrived, I'd just gotten out of the shower. I'd oiled my body down and was waiting patiently for him to make his way to me again.

Spreading my legs wide, I rubbed slowly over my wet pussy lips and bit my bottom lip. "Fuck me, Quinton," I moaned.

I couldn't wait to show him how good I could hit a few high notes.

———

IN THE MIDDLE of the night, I woke up alone. I smoothed my hand over the comforter of my queen-sized bed and sighed.

Quinton's warmth was missing.

Because of how connected I felt to him, I knew he wasn't far. I didn't feel alone, and my house felt like more than a home with him around.

On my way to get a bottle of water from the fridge, I found him. He was in the kitchen sitting around the center island. His laptop was open, and a container of peanut butter cookies was sitting next to it. I giggled at the glass of almond milk sitting beside it all. He had my jug of unsweetened almond milk sitting out, too.

He'd really made himself at home, and I didn't have any complaints about it.

"Working?" I kissed his back, then walked around him to the fridge.

"Yeah, I'm behind on these emails," he said, clicking away. "The emails never stop with this position. Got a lot of team leads hitting me up about shit they can use their common sense to solve."

"Now why would they do that when they can just email you for the answers?"

"Aye, don't come in here with all that."

I laughed and swiped a cookie from the container I'd put up for him. "How do you like them? I tried a new from scratch recipe I found on Pinterest."

"They're always good as fuck to me."

Music to my ears.

"Tell me something," I blurted. "What do you desire to do, Quinton? I mean, since I've known you, all you've done is progress, but what's your passion, businessman?" I asked and blushed. His strong work ethic was inspiring and a turn on.

"That's it," he said and stood from the stool. He snatched me into him and held onto me like I was going somewhere. "I don't think too deeply into things. Progression is all I'm after."

Quinton was a simple man who deserved it all—a thoughtful man who was just for me.

"In the meantime, I'm passionate about you," he spoke against my lips. "And I'm glad we're progressing. I love you, Jana."

"I love you too, Quinton Finch."

EPILOGUE

AND THAT WAS ONLY the beginning of our love story.

"And that was only the beginning of our love story," I repeated aloud.

My therapist scribbled something on her notepad with a red ink pen. I hated that damn notepad! She wrote hard and quick on it anytime I took a short break from speaking. Sometimes I wanted to know what she was writing down about me, but then again, I knew I wouldn't be able to handle her notes. Shit, I could barely handle the unbiased feedback she threw at me every two weeks. She was innocent and only doing her job, but I was overly sensitive and my own worst critic.

Looking up from her notepad, she smiled at me

and shifted in her seat a bit. "So, you let him in," she said, and I nodded.

"Isn't that what you suggested?"

"It is, but not just for love. What you two are building together seems beautiful and healthy right now, and that's great. But I believe you were scared of him because he challenges you to be the best you that you can be. Not only does he make you feel in ways you've never felt before, he motivates you to be great." She leaned back in her velvet, padded high-back chair and repositioned her glasses on her face. "I bet that makes you feel out of control."

She got me. She really, really got me.

"Yes! Exactly, Deja. I don't like that feeling. It flares my anxiety." I rolled my eyes, and Deja snickered.

Deja Williams was the first therapist I ever had and as real as it got. Confidence poured out of her. Her head was always high, her brown skin always glowed, and she knew how to pick a situation apart until we got down to the bottom of it. She was a woman of solution and I was grateful Molli had suggested her to me.

Deja didn't hold back with me and I needed that type of honesty in my life.

"We've been seeing each other for a while.

During our time together, I've gathered that you prefer being in control."

"Oop. Gather me then," I quipped.

Like I said, Deja kept it real.

"There's nothing wrong with being in control. You go for what you want. You do what you love. You fight for what's right. That's the great part about it. But, well, you already know what I'm going to say next. I tell you this every other week."

"Yeah, I know. I can't control everything," I mumbled to myself and circled my fingers around my jeans. I crossed my legs, then uncrossed them again. Facing the truth wasn't that easy for me.

I managed to tuck my curls behind my ears and face her again, but not before looking out of the floor to ceiling window in her immense, plush office. We were fifteen floors up and it was raining. The rain was pelting down, tapping the window at a peaceful rhythm.

"I think you've learned a lot about yourself over the last two weeks. Last time we spoke, Quinton was your boss who you wanted to stop sleeping with."

I burst into laughter and slapped my knee. "Life comes at you fast doesn't it?"

I couldn't deny Quinton's presence in my life

anymore. He'd come into my world and changed my perspective on love, life and everything in between.

No more denying that I was thankful for him, and madly in love with him, too.

"It does, especially when the stars align and it's meant to be," Deja said.

"Yes, especially when the stars align and it's meant to be," I repeated her sentiment, then shrieked with laughter behind my hands.

The End

AUTHOR'S NOTE

Thank you for reaching the end of Jana's story. If you've enjoyed this book, please consider leaving a review on Amazon + Goodreads

Here are some goodies to enjoy: Impassioned Intentions' Apple Music Playlist: https://music.apple.com/us/playlist/impassioned-intentions/pl.u-zPyLLR3tEdop6E

Impassioned Intentions' Pinterest Board: https://pin.it/6ArsvgL

Join us in my readers group on Facebook to share your thoughts on *Impassioned Intentions*: http://bit.ly/ShaniceRomanticHaven

You can also connect with me on my personal Facebook here: http://bit.ly/FBShaniceSwint

To be the first to know of new releases, cover

reveals, giveaways and more, subscribe to my mailing list here: http://eepurl.com/dsb1EL

Again, thank you so, so much for indulging in Jana's story! I can't wait to hear from you.

xoxo, ShanicexLola